Graham S. Morrison

Oxford University Press
Music Department, Walton Street, Oxford OX2 6DP

Contents

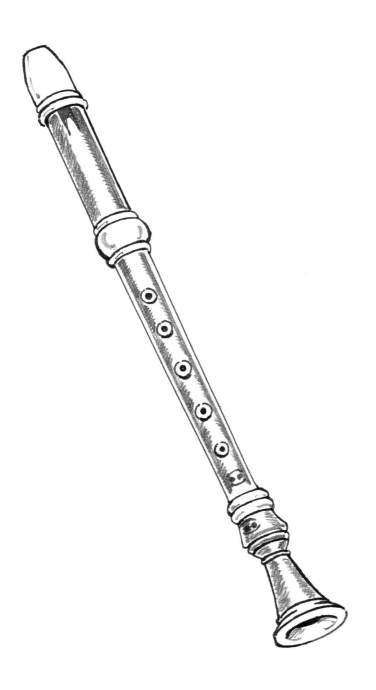

Some simple rules

1 The first three fingers of the *left* hand cover the top three holes of the recorder, nearest the mouthpiece.
The left thumb covers the hole at the back.
The four fingers of the *right* hand cover the bottom four holes, with the right thumb supporting the recorder from underneath, opposite the second hole.

2 Use the soft part at the end of each finger to cover the holes; *not* the very tips of the fingers.

3 Don't drop, heat, bite your recorder or allow it to roll on to the floor. This may prove fatal!
The lip is fragile, so protect it.

4 Clean the inside of the recorder with a cleaning brush or cloth after use.

Playing the note B

1 Holding the recorder in the position shown in the picture, cover the left thumbhole and the left first. Support the recorder with your right thumb, but keep all other fingers clear of the holes.

2 Without the recorder in your mouth, practise whispering 'too' 'too' 'too' very gently. This is called **tonguing**. It helps you to separate one note from the next.

3 Now, still covering the left thumbhole and the left first, place the tip of the mouthpiece on the middle of your bottom lip and close your top lip over it. Just take the tip of the mouthpiece into your mouth, without it touching your teeth.

4 Take a breath and whisper four 'too's' into the recorder. You have now played four Bs. Practise them until you can play four clear Bs every time.

Fingering Chart B

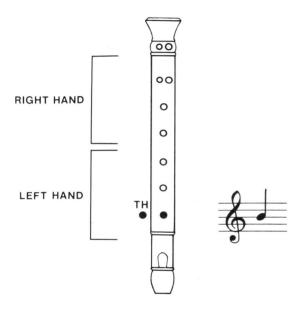

RIGHT HAND

LEFT HAND

TH

One-beat notes (crotchets); bar-lines

1 In most tunes some notes last longer than others, so we have to write different signs for each different length of note.

2 Notes which last for **one beat** are given this sign ♩ or 𝄽 and are called **crotchets**. The four Bs you played in lesson one would be written

B   B   B   B

3 If you played four groups of these four Bs, they would be written

B   B   B   etc.

Each group of four notes is separated from the next by vertical lines called **bar-lines**. At the end of the tune we put a double bar-line. This tune has four beats in a bar.

4 Let's play the tune. Remember to whisper 'too' for each note. The comma indicates where you are to take a breath.

B   B   etc.

Two-beat notes (minims)

1 Notes which last for **two beats** are written ♩ or ♭ and are called **minims**. To play a two-beat note you whisper *one* long 'too' into the recorder, letting the note sound for two beats. Try playing four two-beat notes using the note B.

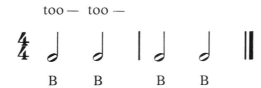

2 Now let's use two-beat and one-beat notes in the same tune.

Notice that each bar still adds up to four beats.

3 In this tune the note lengths have been mixed up even more. Use the rhythms of the football team names to help you with the rhythms of the awkward bars.

Fingering Chart A

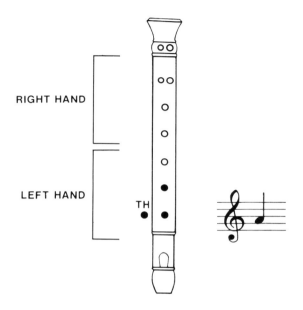

RIGHT HAND

LEFT HAND

TH

A new note – A

1 Hold the recorder in the correct position and cover the left thumbhole and left first. Now play four one-beat notes ♩ ♩ ♩ ♩ . What note have you just played?

2 Still covering the fingering for B, add your left second finger. This is the fingering for the note A. Let's play this tune using the note A. Remember Raith Rovers?

too — too too

A A A A etc.

3 Now try playing three Bs followed by three As in this rhythm ♩ ♩ ♩ . Does Swansea Town ring a bell?

Only your left second finger moves. Your left thumb and first finger stay in their places.

B B B   A A A

4 See if you can work out the fingering and rhythm of this simple tune. Practise it now on your own.

B B B   A A A   B B A A   A   B

Three tunes using B and A

1 Try clapping the rhythm first. Then play the tune.

B B A   A A B   B   A   A A B

2 This is the sign for a four-beat note ○ called a **semibreve**.
Whisper *one* long 'too' into the recorder, letting the note sound for four beats. *Think* when you come to the last bar of this tune.

B   B   A   A A   B B A A   B

3 Try this tune without the teacher's help!

B A B A   A   B   B A A A   B

Fingering Chart G

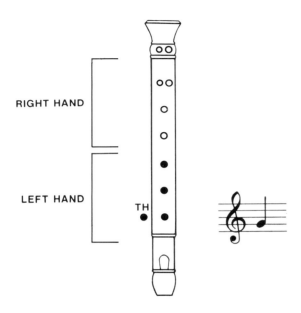

RIGHT HAND

LEFT HAND

A new note – G

1 Hold the recorder in the correct position and play three notes on A in this rhythm.

A   A   A

2 Now add your left third finger and using the same rhythm, play three notes on G.

G   G   G

3 Play four groups in this rhythm, using the note G. Check that you are fully covering the holes, as the smallest gap can produce the wrong note.

G   G   G etc.

4 Still using the same rhythm, play the notes B A G.

Remember to whisper 'too' for each note.

too too too —

B A G   B A G   B A G   B A G

Three tunes using B A G

1

B B A   G G A   B   A   B A G

2 Practise the jump from B to G in the third bar, until you can play it without any extra sounds between the two notes. Your left second and third fingers must move up and down as if they were stuck together.

B   A G G   A   B G B G   A   G

3 Don't lift your fingers too far above the holes. 2 cms is quite enough. Too much movement stops you playing quick notes. You might even miss the hole!

G A B A G B   B G B A G

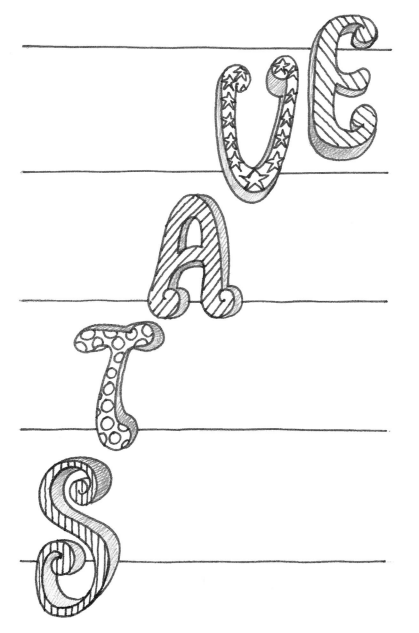

Reading from the stave

1 Music for descant recorder is written on five *lines* and four *spaces* called a **stave**.

2 If you think of the stave as a ladder with five steps and four spaces in between, then the high notes are at the top and the low notes are at the bottom.

High

Low

3 The notes can either sit in the *spaces*

or on the *lines* with the line going through the middle of the head of the note. They are always numbered from the bottom upwards.

With two-beat notes they look like this.

Spaces      **Lines**

4 The stems of the notes below the middle (third) line go *up*. The stems of the notes above the middle line go *down*. The middle line stems can go either *up* or *down*.

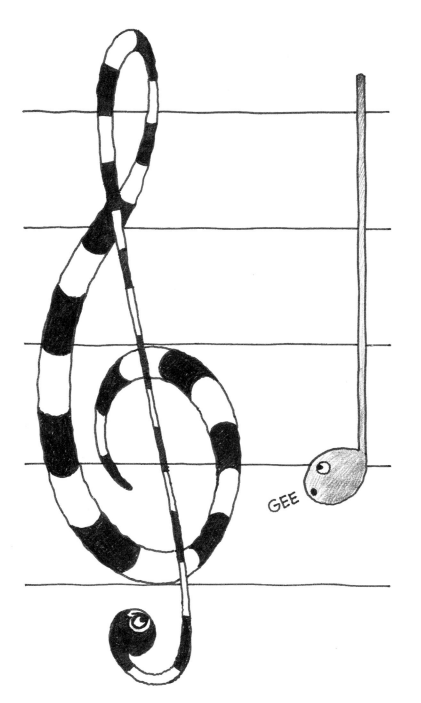

Finding B A G on the stave

1 The **treble** or **G clef**  is placed at the beginning of the stave and tells us that the music written on that stave is for reasonably high-sounding voices or instruments, for example, trumpet, recorder or flute. The treble clef also tells us that G is the *second line*, because it curls round the second line. That is why it is sometimes called the G clef.

2 The next note up by step from G is A (check this by playing G – A). We place A in the *second space*.

3 By playing G A B on the recorder, we find that B is the next note up by step from A. We place B on the *third line*.

Two or more of you could play these rhythms while the rest play the tunes.

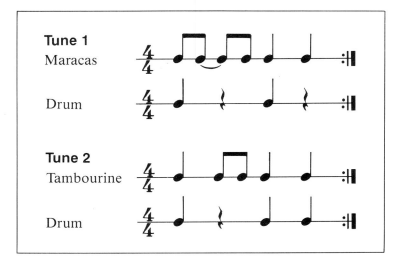

Two tunes to read from the stave

1 Read the letter names of the notes out loud first, then play the first four bars. The second half is almost the same. Remember to count four beats on these notes o .

2 The rhythm in the third and fourth bars is easy if you use the words 'We *are* the best'. Try saying and clapping it first, *Moderato* means that the tune must be played at a moderate pace.

Half-beat notes (quavers)

1 The rhythm in bars 1 and 2 and bars 5 and 6 fits the chant 'We are the champions'. Remember to move your second and third fingers together for the jump from B to G.

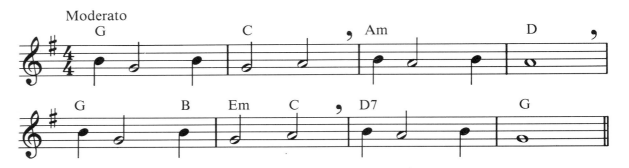

2 Two half-beat notes (*quavers*) are written like this ♫ or ♫ . When two half-beat notes are used in a tune along with one-beat notes, they are played exactly twice as fast.

3 Try clapping these short rhythms. The football names will help you.

a) West - ham U - ni - ted

b) Tot - ten - ham Hot - spur

c) Man - che - ster U - ni - ted

d) Slo - van Bra - ti - sla - va

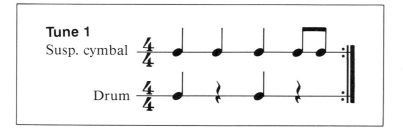

Tune 1
Susp. cymbal
Drum

Two tunes using half-beat notes

Before playing, say the letter names out loud, then clap the rhythm.

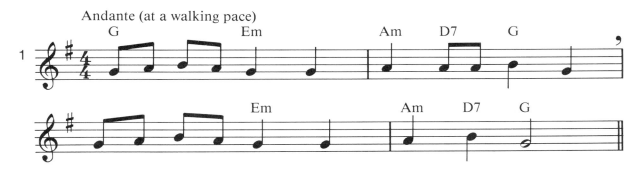

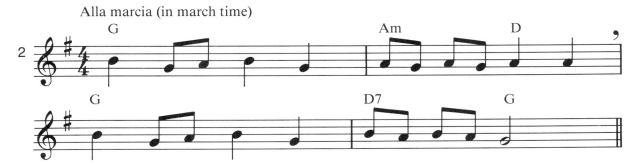

Tune 1
Triangle

Drum

Tune 2
Tambourine

Drum

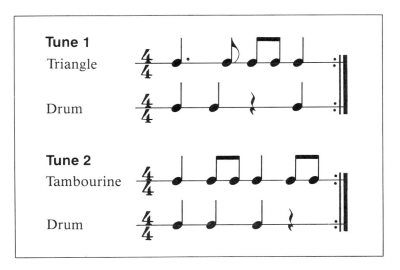

Fingering Chart E

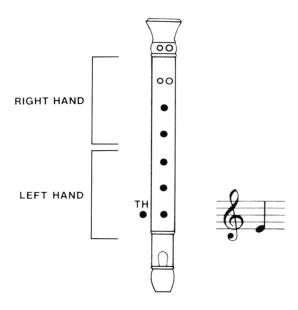

RIGHT HAND

LEFT HAND

TH

A new note – E

1 Holding the recorder in the correct position, cover the fingering for the note G. Now add the first two fingers of the *right* hand. This is the fingering for E. The note E is written on the bottom line.

E

2 Now, gently, using the sound 'doo' which is slightly softer than 'too', play six Es as shown below.

3 Practise this simple exercise, moving to E from different notes. Remember not to lift your fingers too far above the holes.

Adagio (slow)

Two tunes using E

1 Remember to use the softer 'doo' sound for the Es.

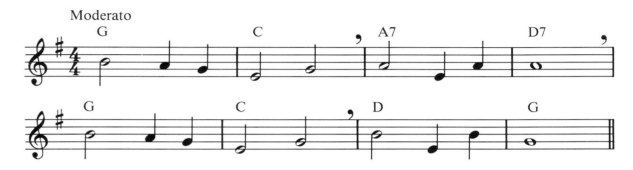

2 Practise the fourth bar several times before trying the rest of the tune.

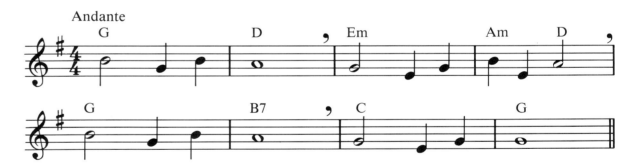

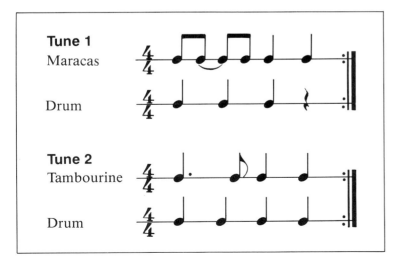

Three-beat notes; waltz-time

1 When we write tunes with three beats in a bar instead of four, we create a totally new rhythm.

2 Let's try an experiment. We'll take *twelve* one-beat notes and group them as four beats in a bar. Clap the rhythm putting an accent (>) on the first beat of each bar.

Now clap them grouped as three beats in a bar, again accenting the first beat of each bar.

Notice the difference?

3 We will also use a three-beat note in waltz-time.
It looks like a two-beat note with a dot placed after it.

♩. = three-beat note

The dot adds half the value of the note it is placed after.

e. g. ♩. = ♩ + . = $1\frac{1}{2}$ beats
          (1) $(\frac{1}{2})$

     o. = o + . = 6 beats
         (4)   (2)

Two waltzes

1 The last two bars contain a tied note G. This means that the note is only sounded once, but lasts for the value of both three-beat notes added together. It therefore becomes a note lasting for six beats.

Tune 1
Susp. cymbal

Drum

Tune 2
Susp. cymbal

Drum

Fingering Chart D

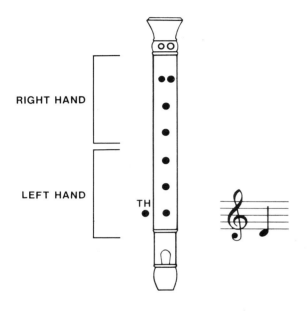

RIGHT HAND

LEFT HAND

TH

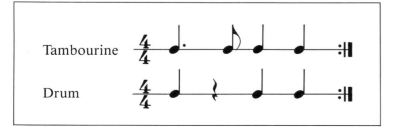

Tambourine

Drum

A new note – D

1 Holding the recorder in the correct position, cover the fingering for the note E. Now add the third finger of your right hand. Be careful to cover both parts of this double-hole. This is the fingering for the note D, which sits *below* the bottom line.

D

2 Now gently, again using the sound 'doo', play ten Ds as shown below.

3 Practise this exercise in moving to D from different notes.

Moderato

Two tunes using D

In both these tunes the rhythm will need to be learned by imitation. You must listen carefully to your teacher when the tunes are demonstrated.

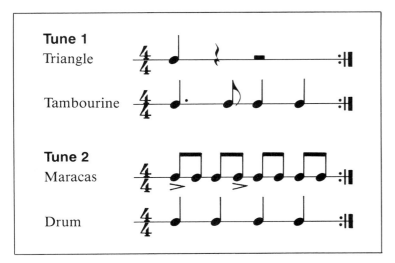

Tune 1
Triangle

Tambourine

Tune 2
Maracas

Drum

Rests and a pop tune

1 In most music **rests** are needed. These are periods of silence, which may be to allow you to breathe or simply to make a change from continuous music.
Rests can be short, for example, a half-beat rest

or long, for example, a four-beat rest.

2 Here is a table of some of the rests you may be using in future lessons. You can refer back to it when necessary.

    4 beat   2 beat   1 beat Two ½ beat

3 ## Hello, this is Joanie

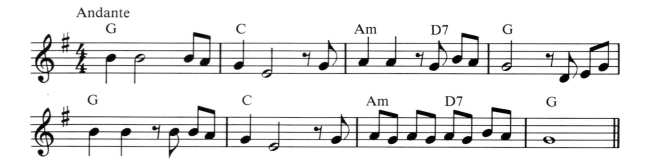

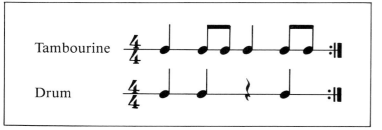

Fingering Chart C

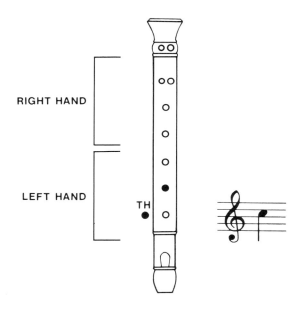

RIGHT HAND

LEFT HAND

TH

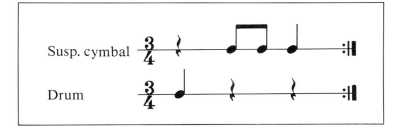

Susp. cymbal

Drum

A new note – C

1 Holding the recorder in the correct position, cover the fingering for the note A. Play this exercise.

Now remove your left first finger. This leaves you with your left second finger and thumb covering their holes and this is the fingering for the note C, which sits in the third space. Play these Cs.

2 Try this simple tune which always brings in the note C after the note A, so you only have to lift your left first finger to move from A to C.

Allegretto (Slightly slower than allegro)

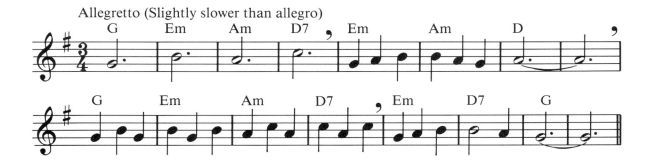

Two more tunes using C

1 Learn the rhythm of this tune by imitation.

2 Notice the one-beat rests at the beginning of several bars. Count *one* in to yourself at the beginning of each of these bars. The accompaniment plays a chord during each of the recorder rests. The bracketed notes marked 1 are only played the first time. When you reach this repeat sign :‖ you must go back to the beginning. The second time through you miss out the ☐1 bracket and play the ☐2 bracket.

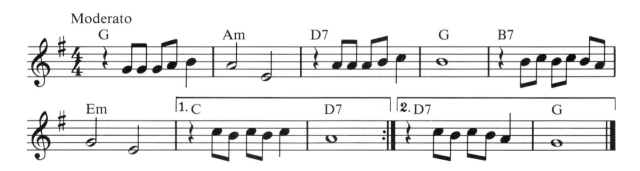

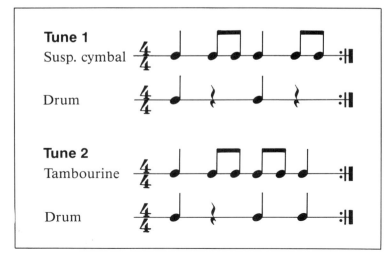

Fingering Chart High D

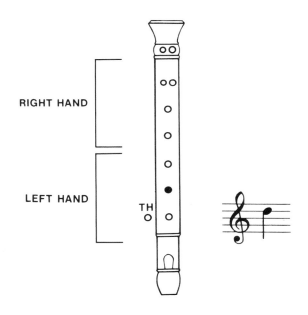

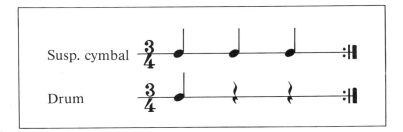

A new note – high D (D′)

1 Holding the recorder in the correct position, cover the fingering for the note C. Be careful to have your right thumb in position to support the recorder and have the mouthpiece between your lips. Now, by simply lifting off your *left* thumb, leaving only the left second finger, you have the fingering for the note high D which sits on the fourth line. To stop you from getting mixed up with the D you have already learned, we show high D like this – D′.

2 Play this exercise moving from C to high D.

3 Annie's song

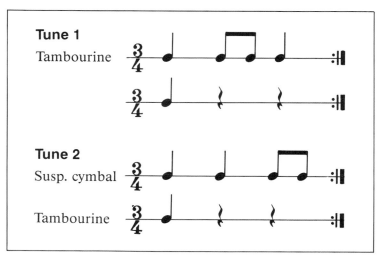

Two more pop tunes using high D

1 The notes written are called **triplets**. Each note is equal to $\frac{1}{3}$ of a beat.

Amazing grace

2 When playing the low Ds which are half-beat notes, make sure that the notes sound properly. Listen carefully to the rhythms of bars 5 and 9; your teacher will play them to you.

When I need you

Fingering Chart F Sharp

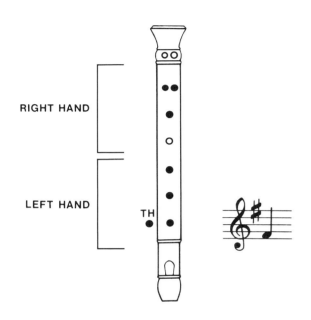

RIGHT HAND

LEFT HAND

TH

A new note – F sharp (F♯)

1 Holding the recorder in the correct position, cover the fingering for the note G. Now add your *right* second and third fingers. This is the fingering for the note F sharp which sits in the first space.
When we use F sharp instead of just F, we must put a sharp sign (♯) at the beginning of the tune, to tell us that every time we come across a note in the first space we will have to use the fingering for F sharp not F. The sharp sign is placed on the fifth line, which is high F.

2 Try playing this exercise.

3 Now try this tune. When you reach the repeat sign you must go back to the beginning and play up to the *Fine* bar.

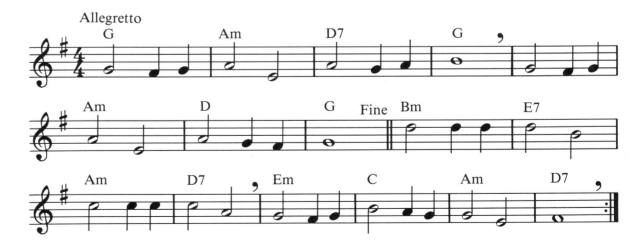

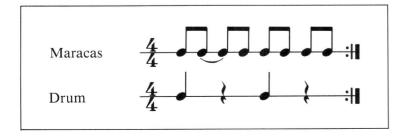

Maracas

Drum

Two pop tunes using F sharp

1 Before you play this tune, practise moving from E to F sharp.

Can't help falling in love

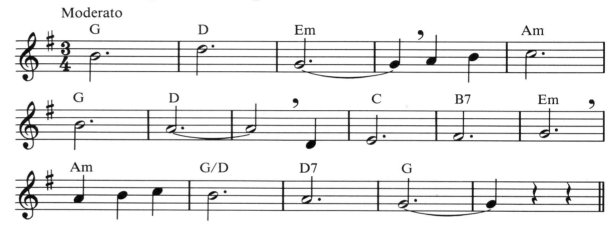

2 Listen carefully when your teacher plays the rhythm in bar 9.

Love me tender

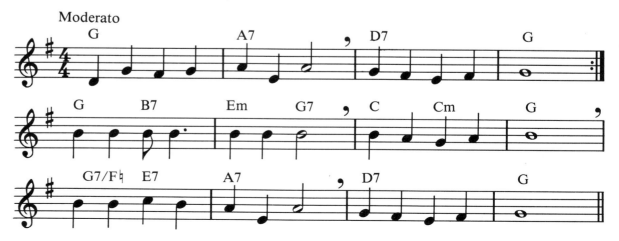

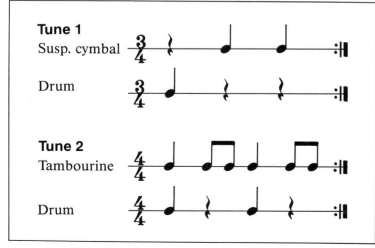

Tune 1
Susp. cymbal

Drum

Tune 2
Tambourine

Drum

Some of the rhythms in the second half of this tune are tricky: your teacher will demonstrate them.

Streets of London

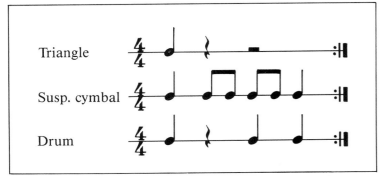

Another pop tune using F sharp

You will have to learn the rhythm of this tune by imitation so listen carefully to your teacher. You will probably know the tune. It comes from the musical *Evita* by Andrew Lloyd Webber.

Don't cry for me Argentina

Fingering Chart C Sharp

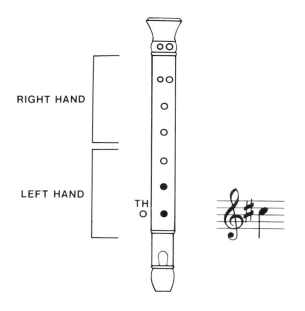

RIGHT HAND

LEFT HAND

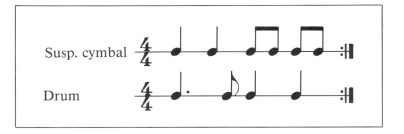

Susp. cymbal

Drum

A new note — C sharp (C#')

1 Holding the recorder in the correct position, cover the fingering for high D. Now simply add your left first finger and you have the fingering for C sharp. Again we have to use the sharp sign (#) at the beginning of each tune in which C is to be sharpened.

2 Play this exercise.

3 Now learn this tune.

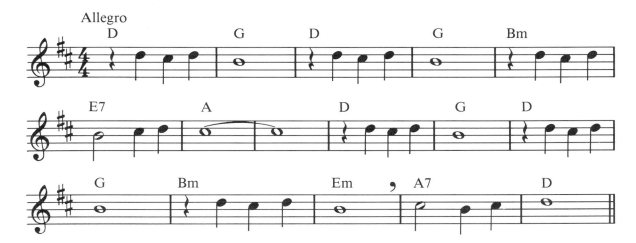

Two pop tunes using C sharp

1 Listen carefully to the rhythm in bars 5 and 15 when your teacher plays you the tune.

Mr Tambourine Man

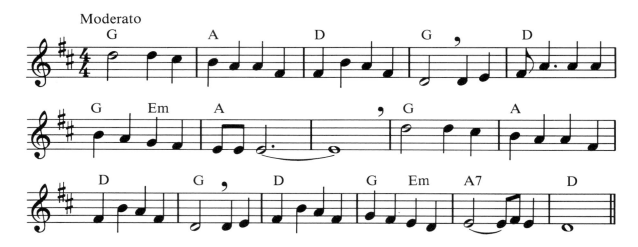

2 Learn this tune by imitation. It has some very tricky rhythms. Notice at the beginning of the tune the F sharp and C sharp signs.

Tijuana taxi

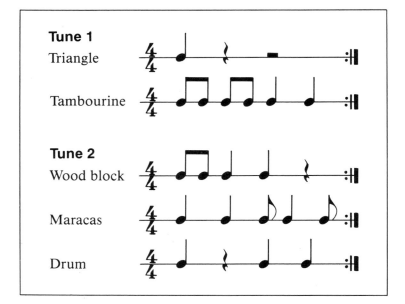

Fingering Chart High E

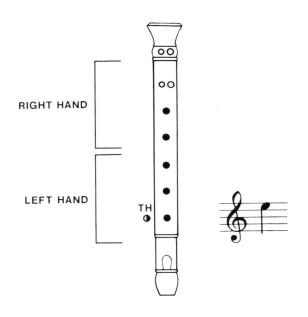

RIGHT HAND

LEFT HAND

TH

A new note — high E (E')

1 Holding the recorder in the correct position, cover the fingering for low E. Now move your left thumb slightly to the left and bend it so that the tip of your thumbnail is placed in the hole. This leaves a small gap and is called **pinching**. This is the fingering for the note E′; it sits in the fourth space.

2 Play this exercise just by moving your left thumb.

3 # Portsmouth

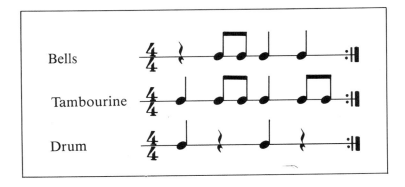

Two well known tunes using high E

1 Scarborough Fair

2 Morning has broken

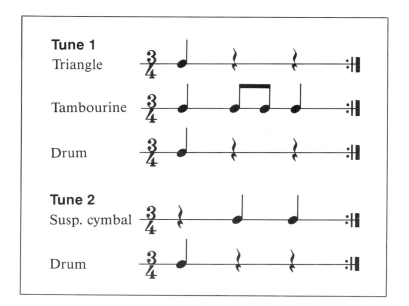

Tune 1
Triangle

Tambourine

Drum

Tune 2
Susp. cymbal

Drum

Two more pop tunes to learn

1 Sailing

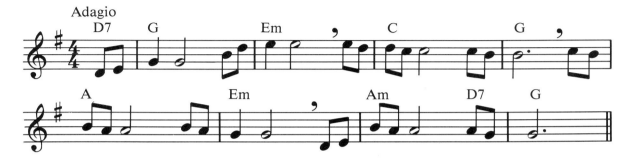

2 Mull of Kintyre

Tune 1
Susp. cymbal

Tambourine

Tune 2
Triangle

Drum

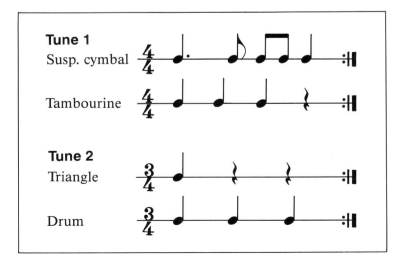

In this tune there are several low Ds which are only half-beat notes. Practise them careful-ly, tonguing gently, to ensure the notes are sounding properly.

A Jamaican song

Mango walk

Fingering Chart F

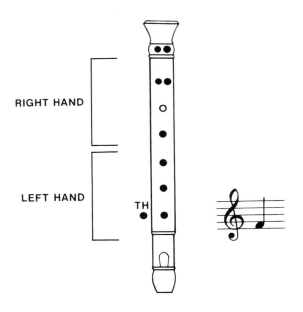

A new note – F (or F natural, F♮)

1 Holding the recorder in the correct position, cover the fingering for the note G. Now add your right first, third and fourth fingers. This is the fingering for F or F natural, which sits in the first space.

2 Play this exercise.

3 Now try this tune. Notice the natural signs (♮) which have been put in to cancel out the sharp sign at the beginning. When notes are altered specially in this way, they are called **accidentals**.

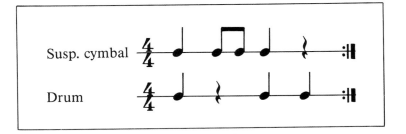

LESSON 35

A tune using F.

Chopsticks

Vivace (Fast, lively)

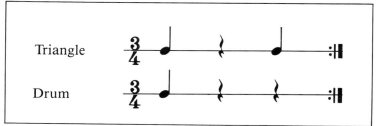

Triangle

Drum

Two more tunes using F

1 Learn the rhythm of this tune by imitation.

2 **Edelweiss**

(from *The Sound of Music*)

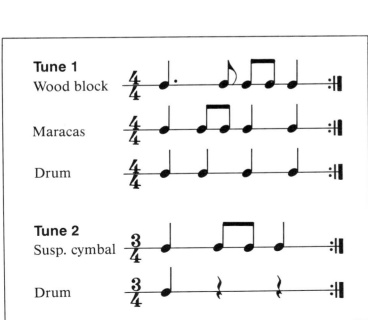

Tune 1
Wood block

Maracas

Drum

Tune 2
Susp. cymbal

Drum

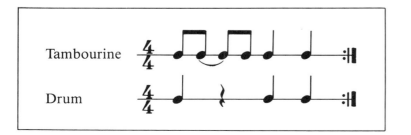

A lesson to help you play G F♮ E

Practise these two exercises carefully before you try to play the next tune.

Puff the magic dragon

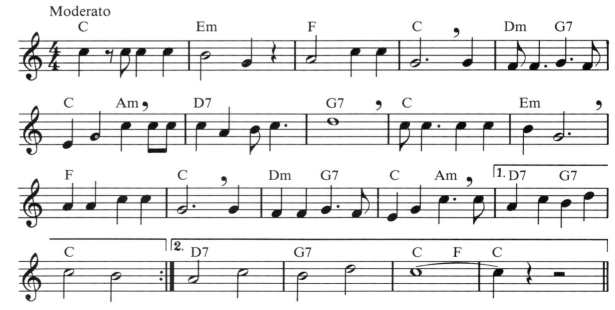

Fingering Chart Middle C

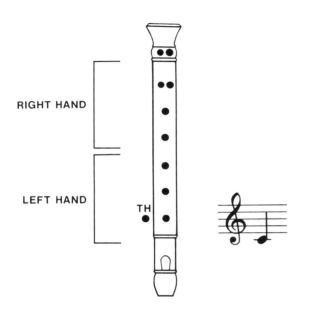

RIGHT HAND

LEFT HAND

TH

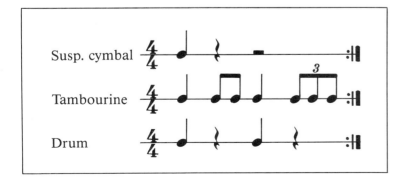

Susp. cymbal				
Tambourine				
Drum				

A new note – middle C

1 Holding the recorder in the correct position, cover all the holes. This is the fingering for middle C. It is called middle C because it lies on its own line (**leger line**) between the treble and the bass staves. You must breath very gently using the sound 'doo'.

2 Approach middle C by downward steps using this exercise.

3 Now, on your own, practise playing several middle Cs. Remember to breath gently using 'doo'. Check that all the holes are fully covered with the fingers fairly flat. If you have problems playing middle C, go back to exercise 2 and repeat it until you are ready to go on.

4 I believe

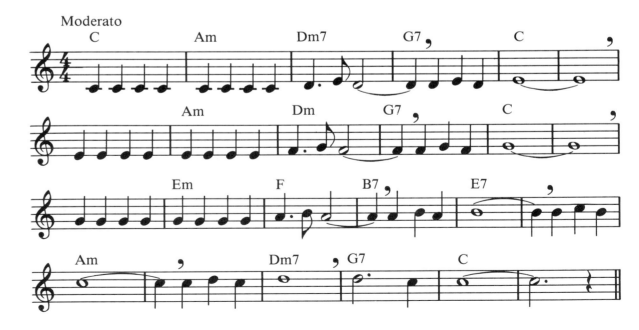

A tune ending on middle C

In this tune try to hold the four-beat notes for almost their full length, just allowing half a beat to breathe before the next phrase.

Morningtown ride

Two more tunes using middle C

1 We shall overcome

Alla marcia

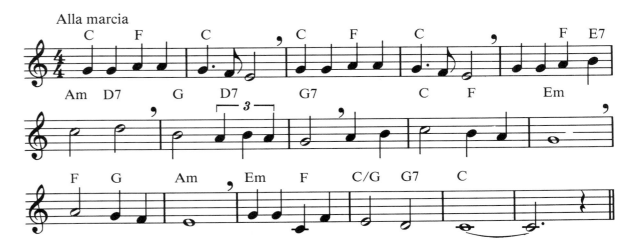

2 Floral dance

Allegro vivace

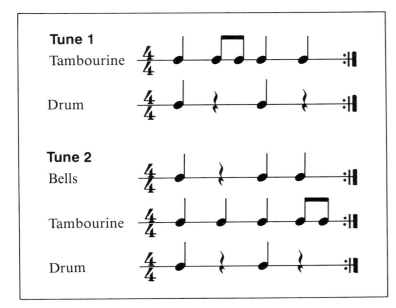

Tune 1
Tambourine

Drum

Tune 2
Bells

Tambourine

Drum

Fingering Chart B Flat

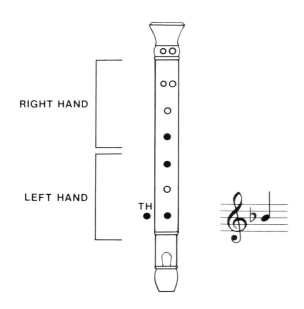

A new note – B flat (B♭)

1 Holding the recorder in the correct position, cover the left thumb, first and third fingers and the right first finger. This is the fingering for B flat. It is written on the third line with a flat sign (♭). If you see B flat placed at the beginning of the tune this means that all the Bs in the tune have to be B flat.

2 Play these B flats.

3 Plaisir d'amour

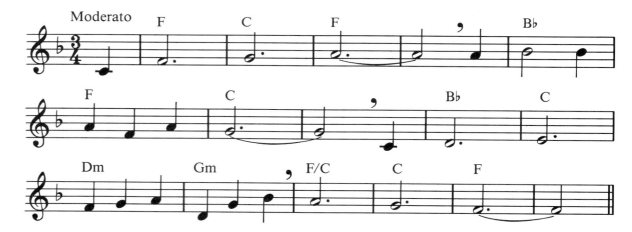

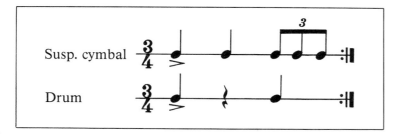

Two more tunes using B flat

1 Please release me

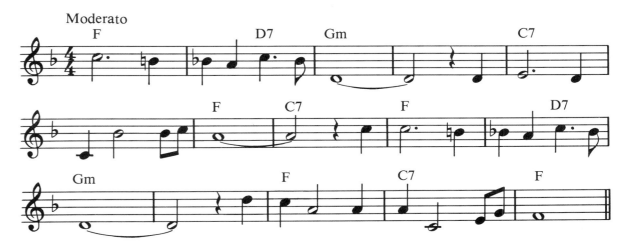

2 When the saints go marchin' in

Tune 1
Wood block

Tambourine

Drum

Tune 2
Tambourine

Drum

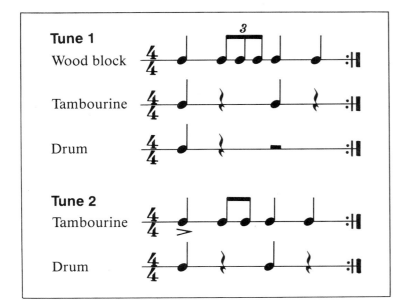

Fingering Chart High F

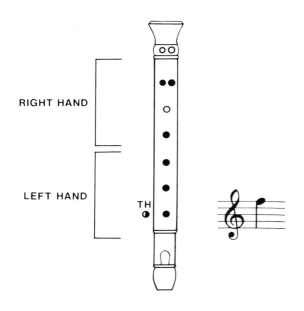

Triangle				
Maracas				
Drum				

A new note — high F (F′)

1 Holding the recorder in the correct position, cover the *left* first, second and third fingers and 'pinch' the thumbhole. Also cover the *right* first and third fingers. This is the fingering for the note F′, which sits on the top (fifth) line.

2 Play this exercise moving from F′ to E′.

3 Now try this tune. Notice the B flat at the beginning.

All my loving

More practice for high F

Now try these exercises.

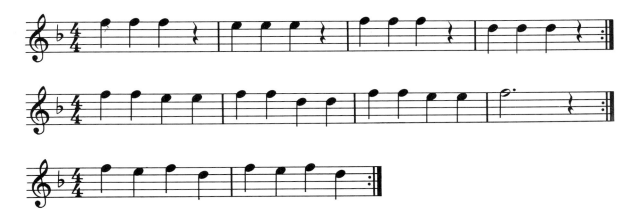

Match of the day

Another tune using high F

Sing

Fingering Chart Middle C Sharp

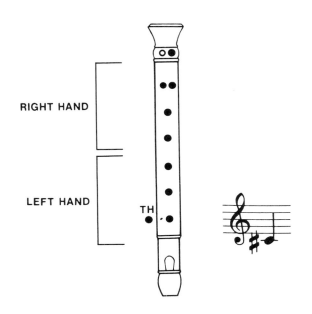

RIGHT HAND

LEFT HAND

TH

A new note — middle C sharp (C♯)

1 Holding the recorder in the correct position, cover the fingering for middle C. Now slide your right fourth finger downwards until one of the two holes is open. This is the fingering for middle C sharp.

2 Try this exercise. Notice that F and C are sharpened by the two sharp signs at the beginning of the stave.

3 Now, try this tune.

Blowing in the wind

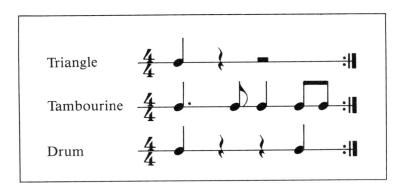

Another tune using middle C sharp

The surrey with the fringe on top

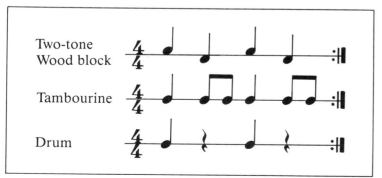

Fingering Chart G Sharp

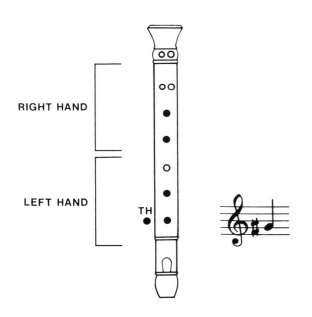

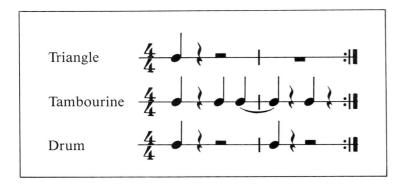

Triangle	
Tambourine	
Drum	

A new note – G sharp (G♯)

1 Holding the recorder in the correct position, cover the fingering for the note A. Now add your right first and second fingers. This is the fingering for the note G sharp.

2 Play this exercise. Notice that once a note has been sharpened or flattened, the sharp or flat applies throughout that bar, unless it is cancelled out by a natural sign.

3 Now try this tune.

Those were the days

Another tune using G sharp

When you play this tune, be careful to tongue the repeated notes accurately.

Catch a falling star

Fingering Chart D Sharp

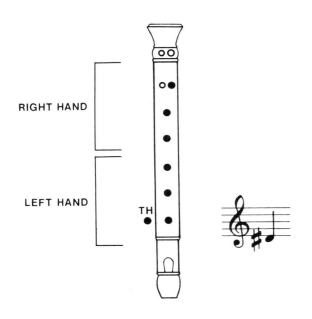

RIGHT HAND

LEFT HAND

TH

Wood block

Tambourine

Drum

LESSON 50

A new note – D sharp (D♯)

1 Holding the recorder in the correct position, cover the fingering for D. Now simply slide your right third finger downwards until one of the two holes is open. This is the fingering for D sharp.

2 Try this exercise.

3 Now play this song from *Oliver*.

I'd do anything

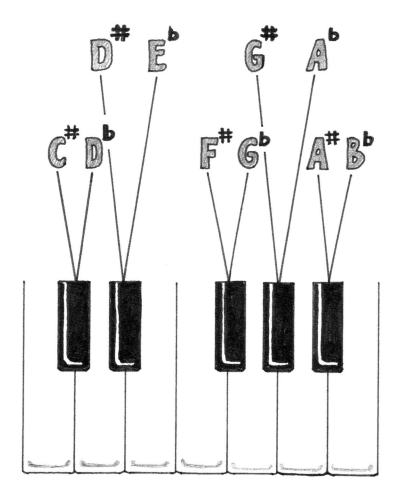

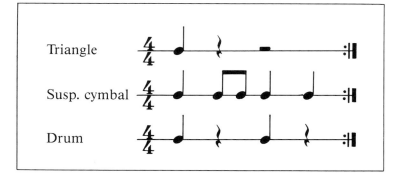

Notes with two names

1 If you look at this picture of part of a piano keyboard you will see that there are black notes between most of the white notes. These black notes are called **sharps** or **flats.**

2 The sharps are one *half* step *higher* than the white notes below them. The flats are one *half* step *lower* than the white notes above them. You will see from the chart that each black note therefore has two names, one *sharp* name and one *flat* name. So C sharp (C♯) is the same as D flat (D♭). Notes that have two names are called **enharmonic** notes.

3 This tune from *Oliver* has the notes A flat and E flat in it. The fingering for A flat is the same as G sharp which you learned in Lesson 48. The fingering for E flat is the same as D sharp in Lesson 50.

Where is love

Fingering Chart High G

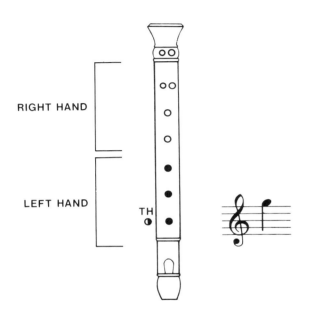

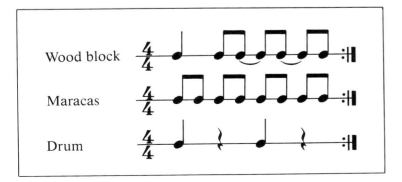

A new note — high G (G′)

1 Holding the recorder in the correct position, cover the fingering for the note G. Now simply pinch the thumbhole. This is the fingering for the note high G or G′, which sits in the space above the top line.

2 Play this exercise.

3 Now try this tune – tongue it very precisely.

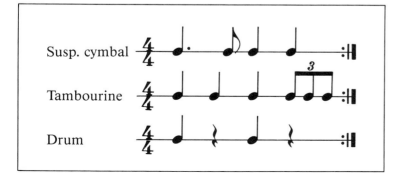

Another tune using high G

You'll never walk alone

Fingering Chart High F Sharp

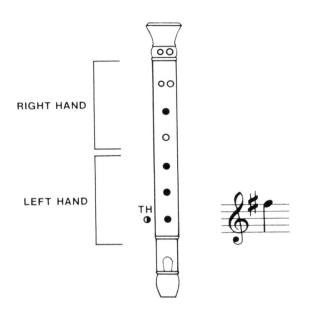

RIGHT HAND

LEFT HAND

Triangle

Maracas

Drum

A new note – high F sharp (F#')

1 Holding the recorder in the correct position, cover the fingering for high G. Now cover your right second finger. This is the finger for F#', which sits on the fifth line.

2 Play this exercise.

3 Now learn this tune.

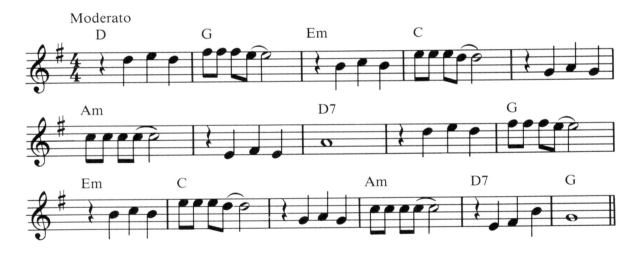

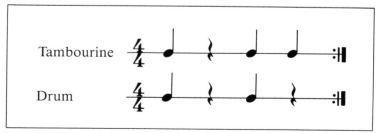

Another tune using high F sharp

Top of the world

Fingering Chart High E Flat

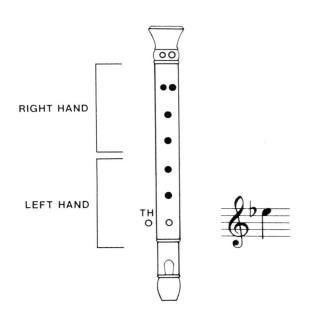

RIGHT HAND

LEFT HAND

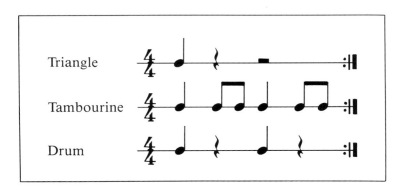

Triangle		
Tambourine		
Drum		

A new note – high E flat (E♭′)

1 Holding the recorder in the correct position, cover your left second and third fingers and right first, second and third fingers. This is the fingering for the note E♭′, which sits in the fourth space.

2 Play these high E flats.

3 # Gonna build a mountain

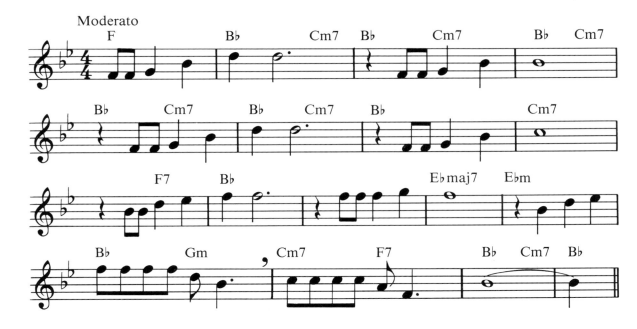

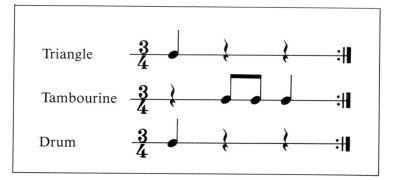

Another tune using high E flat

Sunrise, sunset

Fingering Charts

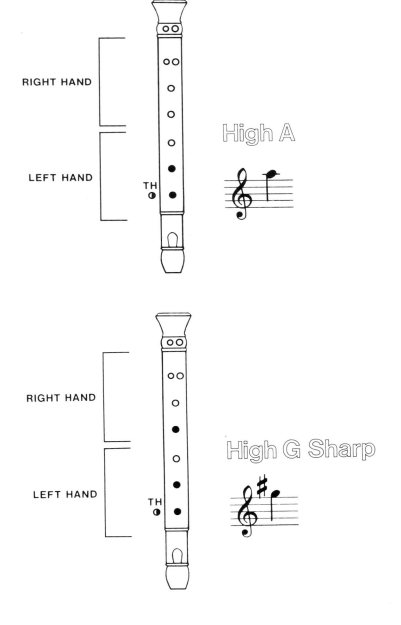

RIGHT HAND

LEFT HAND

TH

High A

RIGHT HAND

LEFT HAND

TH

High G Sharp

Two new notes – high A (A′) and high G sharp (G♯′)

1 Holding the recorder in the correct position, cover the fingering for the note A. Now simply pinch the thumbhole. This is the fingering for high A, which sits on the first **leger** line above the stave.

2 Play this exercise.

3 Holding the recorder in the correct position, cover the fingering for a. Now cover your right first finger. This is the fingering for g′ sharp which sits in the space above the top line.

4 Play this exercise.

A tune introducing high A and high G sharp

Another song from the musical *Oliver*. Notice high D♯ is the same fingering as high E♭.

Food glorious food

A tune using enharmonic notes

This song is sung by the governess in *The sound of music*. Take care with the fingerings of the enharmonic notes E♭ – D♯, A♭ – G♯, D♭ – C♯, and also the naturals.

Doh-re-mi

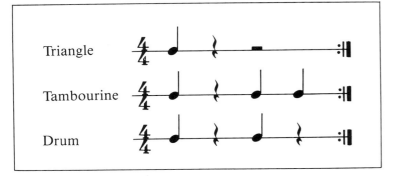

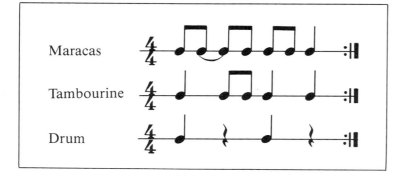

A song with some tricky fingering

Chanson d'amour